SANTA CRUZ PUBLIC LIBRARIES
Santa Cruz, California

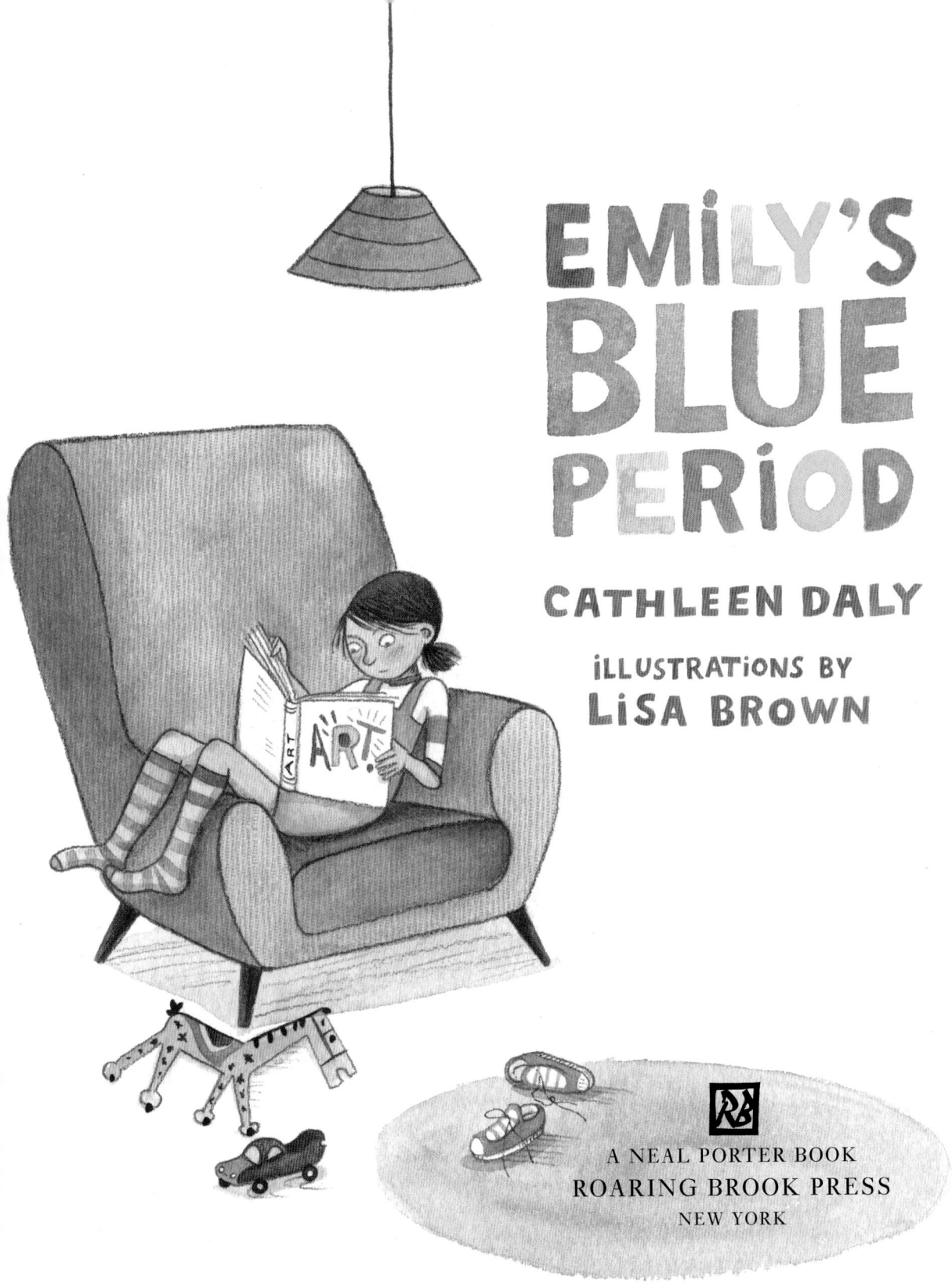


# EMILY'S BLUE PERIOD

CATHLEEN DALY

ILLUSTRATIONS BY
LISA BROWN

A NEAL PORTER BOOK
ROARING BROOK PRESS
NEW YORK

Text copyright © 2014 by Cathleen Daly
Illustrations copyright © 2014 by Lisa Brown
A Neal Porter Book
Published by Roaring Brook Press
Roaring Brook Press is a division of Holtzbrinck Publishing Holdings Limited Partnership
175 Fifth Avenue, New York, New York 10010

The art for this book was created using pencil and watercolor on paper, with some digital collage.
mackids.com
All rights reserved

Library of Congress Cataloging-in-Publication Data
Daly, Cathleen.
Emily's blue period / Cathleen Daly ; illustrated by Lisa Brown. --
First edition.
pages cm
"A Neal Porter Book."
Summary: After her parents get divorced, Emily finds comfort in making
and learning about art.
ISBN 978-1-59643-469-1
[1. Art—Fiction. 2. Divorce—Fiction.] I. Brown, Lisa, 1972-
illustrator. II. Title.
PZ7.D16945Em 2014
[E]—dc23

2013016727

Roaring Brook Press books may be purchased for business or promotional use. For information
on bulk purchases please contact Macmillan Corporate and Premium Sales Department at
(800) 221-7945 x5442 or by email at specialmarkets@macmillan.com.

First edition 2014
Printed in China by Toppan Leefung Printing Ltd., Dongguan City, Guangdong Province

3 5 7 9 10 8 6 4 2

# CONTENTS

CHAPTER ONE • Pablo Picasso . . . . . 5

CHAPTER TWO • All Mixed Up . . . . . 11

CHAPTER THREE • Blue . . . . . 29

CHAPTER FOUR • Collage . . . . . 35

CHAPTER FIVE • Big and Soggy and Beautiful . . . . . 47

This book is dedicated to my family.
—C.D.

To my picture book family: Ashley, Christy, Julie, and Katherine
—L.B.

# CHAPTER ONE

Emily wants to be an

In school Emily is learning about
a famous artist named Pablo Picasso.

PABLO PICASSO
His full name was
Pablo Diego José Francisco de Paula Juan Nepomuceno María de los Remedios Cipriano de la Santísima Trinidad Martyr Patricio Clito Ruiz y PICASSO.

Emily's name is

# EMILY ROSE PINCHNER.

She wants to change it to

So far her parents
won't let her.

Picasso was a cubist.

Sometimes he broke his pictures up into cubes and unusual shapes. Things in his paintings weren't where you'd expect them to be.

He liked to mix things up.

So does Emily.

# CHAPTER TWO

# ~~AX LEMEDIPU~~
# ALL MIXED UP

Lately, Emily's family is mixed up.
She doesn't like this.

Emily's dad is no longer where he belongs.

Suddenly, he lives in his own little cube.

Dad needs to pick out furniture for his new home.

Emily sees little cubes everywhere.

"Do you like this?" asks Dad. It's a soft cube you can put your feet on.

"What about this?"
It's a big square rug.

Everything is pretty, but nothing looks like home.

Really?
Did you know that Pablo Picasso was so poor when he moved to Paris that he couldn't buy furniture?

He painted furniture on his walls so his apartment would feel more homey.
Really!

"WHERE'S JACK?" says Dad a moment later.

JACK!
JACK?

Jack is hiding behind a big couch. He won't come out.

"Come on, Jack," says Dad.
But Jack won't budge.

Jack, come on, we can't sit on this couch forever.
Now Jack won't talk.
No budging and no talking.

He stares at the other busy shoppers. Emily watches, too. Jack is quiet. Dad reaches back and scratches Jack's head.

BIG MISTAKE.

THIS IS MY COUCH FORTRESS AND NO ONE CAN TOUCH ME! NO ARMS ALLOWED IN MY FORTRESS!

Now the shoppers are staring at Dad and Emily.

Dad picks up Jack like a sack of potatoes. They leave the big square store without a thing for Dad's new apartment. Just a silent bag of potatoes that looks like a boy.

CHAPTER THREE

# BLUE

That week Emily's teacher calls her mom.
Mmm hmm, really? That's unusual.
Em, that was your teacher. She said you wouldn't do the art project today. I thought you loved art!
Yes, Mother, I do love art.

Then why didn't you do your project?

"Because we were using charcoal and charcoal is *black*," says Emily.
"What's wrong with black?"
SIGH.
I can't use black because I am in my blue period.
Picasso
Picasso

"When Pablo Picasso was very sad
he only painted in shades of blue.
And now I am in *my* blue period."
It is a little early
in my career to be
having a blue period,
but it is happening
all the same.
Picasso

Emily nuzzles her head into the spot under her mother's arm where it fits just like a puzzle piece.

Emily's Blue Period lasts quite some time.

CHAPTER FOUR

# COLLAGE

One day, Emily learns about collage in art class.

Emily can't wait to try.

Okay, class. I want you to make a collage of your house. You can use anything on this table that reminds you of home.

Emily sits very still. She has two homes. Which one should she make?

She sits and stares at
her blank paper for the
rest of the class.

Mom, is your house or Dad's house my home?
Why, they both are. Why do you ask?

Well, you can't really have two homes can you?
"Why not?" asks Mom. "A lot of people have more than one home."
Home is where the heart is. That's what it says on Billy's mom's potholder.

Emily is quiet all through the rest of dinner. She moves all the different kinds of food on her plate into the shape of a heart before she eats it.

HMMMMM.

After dinner Emily starts digging through things.

The recycling.

Her mother's sewing kit.

The junk drawer.

Like a little animal burrowing here and there. Stashing things away into a little brown bag.

That Saturday she burrows into things at her dad's apartment, too.

The wet bar.

The toolbox.

The top desk drawer.
Then she gets to work.

And work and work.

Cutting and gluing, gluing and cutting some more.

CHAPTER FIVE

# BIG and SOGGY and Beautiful

Finally she is done. It's big and soggy and beautiful. Back at Mom's, Emily hangs the collage up to dry.

"Yep," says Emily. "I mostly make collages now. That's a collage of my home."

"Well, it's not a house, but it's my *home*. It's the home of my heart," says Emily. "See all the stuff from Dad's *and* Mom's plus Jack's head cut out of a photo and Jenny's friendship bracelet and other stuff that shows what's important to me."

I'm glad my head is important to you, Em.

Right before bed, Emily notices a purple blob in the middle of her collage.

Mom and Jack come running.

"It's not a scribble! It's a purple *heart*," says Jack. "I think your collage is the home of my heart, too!"

Emily is remembering what her teacher said about collage.
How you take things from different places to make a whole.

"Really?" says Jack.
"You mean it?"

"Really," says Emily.

And she does.

Now her collage is

PERFECT.

0000122865736